What Comes to Mind?

What Comes to Mind

Published 2025 by Godfrey Coppinger

ISBN: 978-1-916544-72-7

Publishing Information
Publishing & design services
provided by JM Agency

www.jm.agency
Kerry, Ireland

What Comes to Mind?

Stories, Poems and Drawings Inspired by Prompts

Godfrey Coppinger

To the memory of
Geraldine Serpa Chapman
(October 5, 1951 to February 27, 2025)

♥

Though the soul departs
Fifty-six years of friendship
Does not die with death

Introduction

When I moved back to Ireland in 2018, I left behind my California writing group.

I wasn't long here before I was introduced to 'Just Write'. In California we brought whatever we were working on and discussed our work amongst ourselves.

Just Write is a little different. Every two weeks our moderator, Marian Relihan, provides us with a prompt.

I wasn't sure I was going to like this process, but I seldom turn down a challenge, and I tell you – I'm having a blast! The prompts, whether I like them or not, make me think.

I'm still working on stories of my own, but I find that these prompts help me explore many possibilities that I might not have seen otherwise, A case in point is the first prompt we were given when I first joined – Brexit!

No, no, no, I didn't want to write about that. But I did, and I'm actually quite happy with it.

Another was Lake Como. I knew nothing about Lake Como. I looked it up and it's an Italian resort area, not my kind of place at all. But, I did a little more research on the area and – well, read *In the Forest*. It's one of my favourites.

THE RULES

1. We are not allowed to disparage our work, as in "This isn't very good, but..."

2. We can write as much as we want, but can share no more than 500 words with the group – there are at least a dozen of us and

we only have two hours? Many people choose to share parts of longer stories they are working on. Some of the stories are longer because we met on Zoom during Covid and there were fewer people attending.

3. If you don't want to write the prompt you don't have to, but I love seeing the many different directions twelve people can go with one prompt.

4. You don't have to follow the rules. (Except the time limit, but even then...)

I also want to take this opportunity to thank Just Write, a very talented and special group of people who have been my inspiration for the last six years.

THE DRAWINGS

The drawings are also from prompts, mostly. Sometimes the prompt is merely my day-to-day life, or my dreams. I dream a lot. Sometimes I am prompted by something I've read, or seen online.

But during October every year there is a fun challenge called Inktober. Started by Jake Parker in 2009, a prompt is given for each day of the month and you just draw something. There are some rules on the official site, but, generally speaking, I just do what I do.

Mother Britannia's Lament

Alas the world is not as it should be
As when I ruled this terrestrial sphere.
Once I was queen of all across the sea:
I was the one the people did revere.
Now I am mother to the world no more.
My children have rebelled and cast me out.
They don't obey me as they did before.
Now THEY are the ones who think they can shout
And tell me what it is that I must do.
But I will not be told. I am still queen.
I will bid the rebellious world adieu
And rule myself, alone, in quarantine.
I will stand regal in my solitude,
Untouched by this cruel world's ingratitude.

When I first joined the group in 2019, the very first prompt was "Brexit." No! Not a subject I really wanted to write about. But I did it anyway and was quite happy with the result.

August 10, 2020 • This is me cooking enchilada sauce while Lily waits for me to grate cheese
Nopal

The Suitcase

Hazel stood beside the bed dressed in her Sunday best, staring into the suitcase. One suitcase for four people. At least two of the people were small. She smiled at Ruth, who sat on the steps entertaining Carleen with the ragdoll they shared.

The small suitcase contained a change of clothes for each of them; her mother's Bible; four sandwiches; and work clothes, packed with a prayer.

Would there be jobs in California like everyone said? Would oranges be rotting on the ground because they didn't have enough workers to pick them?

She sighed and closed the suitcase, tying a string around it to make sure it stayed closed. She looked around at the dust that covered everything in sight. She was sure there was dust in the suitcase, no matter how hard she tried to keep it out. The dust would probably make it to California even if they didn't.

Carl waited in the yard. He took the suitcase from her. She lifted Carleen into her arms. Ruth held tightly to her skirt as she had been instructed.

Together they disappeared into the dust along the road.

This is a bit of my family's history. In the 1930s during the Great Depression my mama's family hitchhiked from Oklahoma to California. Mama was only three and Aunt Carleen was still an infant.

11 November 2021
Prompts #41 and #42 go together
As long as I have book and a tree, the world is a perfect place

13

At The Top of the Hill

She waited silently at the top of the hill.

Someone would come. If she was patient, they would come.

She was tired of being patient, so tired of being lonely.

Through the woods she could see the cars that passed by on the road below, but none ever ventured up her gravel drive.

Lonely. Bored. Nothing to do. Nobody to care for.

But wait – a car was coming. People. And children! Almost before the car stopped the Boy and the Girl jumped out and ran to get boxes from the boot.

They were moving in.

She almost cried to think she wouldn't be bored anymore. One couldn't be bored with children around.

As the children bounced up the steps she threw her front door open with pure delight.

The girl stopped abruptly. "That was weird."

"Just the wind," said the Mother. "The latch must be broken. It's a very old house."

"Maybe it's haunted," said the Boy.

"Oh no," said The House to herself. "I would never allow ghosts to live here. I would run them off before they even got to the front door."

"Bring in the cleaning supplies," said the Mother, "and the dishes and the pots and pans. We'll get the kitchen set up before we do anything else. "

"I want to pick out my room."

"Me, too!"

The children ran up the stairs.

"This is my room. It will be so pretty when I get it all set up," says the girl.

"Yeah, well it stinks."

"Oh my," thought The House. "He's right. It's been closed up for so long.

.I'd better do something about that."

Both windows flew open.

"MAMA!" The children screamed as they turned and tumbled down the stairs.

"What in heaven's name is wrong with you two."

"The windows opened all by themselves!"

"Don't be silly. Come help us in the kitchen."

As they carried the boxes inside The House thought, "Oh, once again I will hear the clatter of dishes and there will be stories and songs and laughter."

Everyone arrived in the kitchen carrying bags and boxes.

"Oh your hands are full Let me help!" said The House as she threw open all the cupboard doors at once.

15

There was stunned silence. Everyone froze where they stood.

"See, we told you," whispered the Boy.

"I don't like it here," whimpered the Girl. "Do we have to stay?"

Mother and Father looked at each other.

"I think not," they said together

They turned, walking quickly out of The House and down the steps. Jumping into the car they drove off, leaving The House behind

"Wait! Where are you going? Aren't you going to live with me!

If the House had shoulders they would have slumped. If she had eyes they would be filled with tears.

"Why does that always happen?" She sighed. "I was only welcoming them. Why do they always leave?"

At the top of the hill, The House continues to stand, sad and lonely and bored.

I really don't remember what the prompt was for this. It may very well have been "at the top of the hill."

Figuring out the next step
on the rocky road of life.

Ali Baba and the 40 Slugs

Death by Cat

Beyond

With the sunrise behind me
I stand at the edge of the field,
Wondering at the distant mountains.
What is beyond?

With the sunset before me
I beseech the birds
Take me there
Let me fly with you
Over those mountains
And beyond.

In the night
I ask the rising moon,
May I sail on your beams
Across the dark skies
To something more?

As the moon goes down
I see the distant stars
Of the Milky Way
Stretching across the sky,
Stretching across my soul
From then to now
And onward to forever.

The seeds of my soul were planted
In this fertile soil.
My soul grows upwards,
But the roots do not hold
And I must wander.

Perhaps I have no roots
Only wings.

"Beyond" was the prompt.

Monday 14 August 2023

I woke up in the middle of the night and I attempted to count sheep but the sheep were very unruly and wouldn't jump over the fence and some were dancing and others were playing games and most of them were drunk and a fight broke out. I'm tired. I think I'll count hedgehogs next time.

Blankets

Oh, to wrap myself in blankets of words
To snuggle in comfortable phrases
I yearn to stroke the silky borders
Of poems about sunsets and hazes.

If a session ends early, as it often does on Zoom, we are given an extra prompt and a few minutes to write and share. This is such a prompt.

I lay awake last night thinking about my memoir: **From There to Here: An Odyssey of Obstacles**. Got up and started working on it and became immediatley **OVERWHELMED**!

23

The Dragon Riders of Green Gables

Anne and Diana walked arm in arm beside the Lake of Shining Waters. It was a glorious spring day and the two best friends were revelling in the peace of the lovely afternoon.

The peace, however, was suddenly shattered by a shrill cry from the House of Green Gables.

"They're back!" cried Marilla from the porch. "Call the dragons!"

Anne looked to the sky and saw three giant birds of prey approaching from the east. The Venomous Vultures of Val Doucet had returned.

Anne put her fingers to her lips and whistled. From the Haunted Woods there burst two dragons, a gold and a blue. Anne jumped astride the golden dragon and the blue flew to Diana. The dragon riders circled the green-gabled house, then shot into the sky towards the attackers.

Meanwhile Marilla ran inside, up the stairs and onto the roof with her crossbow. Expertly aiming the weapon, she brought down the first of the deadly monsters.

Diana raised her sword and circled one of the beasts, attempting to strike from behind to avoid its poisoned beak. The bird twisted in the air and made a counter attack, but

Diana's blue dragon was too agile and, circling underneath, severed the bird's head with a single swipe of her razor s harp claws.

As Anne flew towards the enemy she threw her hat aside and her fiery hair became a tangle of blazing ropes reaching towards the advancing vulture. The tresses swirled around, above, and below the demon bird, rendering its now tightly bound wings useless, and throwing it into the Lake of Shining Waters to drown.

One shot, one decapitated, and one drowned – it was a good day for the Dragon Riders of Green Gables.

But just when they thought their troubles were over, Marilla called from the house, "Look!!"

From the shores of Nova Scotia, beyond the Strait of Belle Isle, a huge form hurdled towards them, growing larger as it came near.

The ground at their feet shook violently as the Beast of Baddock landed on the cliffs of Prince Edward Island and came bounding towards Avonlea.

"Now!" shouted Marilla from the roof of the house.

In the barn Matthew threw open the hay loft doors and loaded the catapult. Just as the behemoth hurdled itself towards Green Gables, Matthew fired and the Beast of Baddock fell to the ground.

Anne and Diana returned to the House of Green Gables, declaring it a successful day. A celebratory tea was served, after which the residents of Green Gables retired to the veranda to take in the peaceful land before them.

Meanwhile, the faithful dragons carried the body of the Beast of Baddock into the woods where they enjoyed their own feast for many days.

All were well, and happy, and safe.

Until the next time.

This is the kind of prompt I live for! We were tasked with creating a genre mash-up. I had recently re-read Ann McCaffrey's *Dragon Riders of Pern*. I had also read, for the first time (at the age of 70) *Anne of Green Gables*, by Lucy Maud Montgomery. It was the perfect mash-up!

Saturday Inktober 2023
"Sparkle"

Sunday 12 November 2023: Another cycling dream in which its pedal pedal, pedel all night long.

28

Clichés

Once upon a time in a land far away there lived a beautiful princess. Ah, but you can't always judge a book by its cover. Her heart was as ugly as sin and as cold as ice.

Although she was as pretty as a picture, all the princes in the surrounding kingdoms knew of her evil disposition and were definitely not chomping at the bit to ask for her hand in marriage.

But there was one young prince who was as tough as nails and figured that those who told tall tales about the princess were making a mountain out of a molehill.

So, he hopped on his horse and rode into the sunset towards the castle gates. As the sun set the night sky became littered with stars.

At last he came to the home of the princess.

"I have come to ask for the princess's hand in marriage," he announced.

The princess poked her head out of the gate and began to read him the riot act.

"I've had it up to HERE with you stupid princes," she shouted. You're driving me up the wall and I'm sick and tired of it.

"Someone woke up on the wrong side of the bed this morning," said the prince.

"At least I didn't have to share that bed with you," said the princess.

"Let's just nip this argument in the bud," said the prince. "If you marry me I will NOT give you the world. I will NOT fly you to the moon. What I WILL do is share your life. Marry me and every day I will push your buttons. I will drive you up the wall. I will make your blood boil. We will fight like cats and dogs. Please say I do and we will jump the broom."

She did and they did, because the princess had had it up to here with sappy princes wanting her to chase rainbows. She was tired of spitting into the wind.

So, they tied the knot and lived happily ever after making each other miserable.

This is another end-of-session prompt. I think we may have had as much as 15 minutes to complete it. The object was to write a story with as many clichés as we could think of. So much fun!

17 MARCH 2024

Godfrey as Saint Gertrude,
Patron saint of Cats, Travellers,
and Insane People

Prompt: Castle

I am From

I am from
Once upon a time
And long ago.

I am from
A galaxy far, far away,
And from just
Around the corner
And down the street.

I am from Wonderland
And Mulberry street,
From where
The yellow brick road begins
And where the sidewalk ends.

I am from
The wide open plains
Where I run
With coyote through
The sagebrush
And fly with raven
Into the sun.

I am from within
The briar patch
Where I laugh and laugh
With Br'er Rabbit.

I am from African spiders
And Greek goddesses
Chinese dragons
And Norse trolls,
I am from pucas
And chupacabras.

I am from sasquatch
In the forest
And aliens from
Other worlds.

I am from that place
Inside my head
That no one but I can visit.

But I can
Tell you
The story,

Because
I am from
Once upon a time.

George Ella Lyon wrote the poem 'Where I'm From'. It is often used in schools to encourage students to reflect on who they are – what makes them them.

DUET

In the Silence of the Night

Sometimes
In the silence of the night
I consider my demise.
Will I waste away slowly,
In pain, not knowing
Who I am?

Or
Will I die suddenly
With a failing heart
Or a fatal fall?

And when I die
What happens then?
Will I burn forever
In Hell
Because I have not accepted
Someone else's version of
Truth?

Or
Will it be Paradise
Because I have always
Done my best
To be kind to those around me.

And if it should be
Paradise
What will paradise look like?
Will I wander through streets of gold
Stroking my harp and
Wearing an insipid smile?

Perhaps I will be
Born again
To continue the
Learning process
In another life, another body.

Of all the
Possibilities
That would be my preference,
To continue in my
Search
For knowing.

Is that not why we live,
To find The Answers,
To know all, to be all,
To become one with
ALL.

But, of course,
There is another possibility.
Perhaps we simply
Cease,
No more to be.
Perhaps we sink into
Oblivion
For
Eternity.

The prompt was "oblivion". It speaks for itself.

The Traveller

I will imagine myself to be a turtle
Travelling the world with my home on my back
I will meet you at the fair in the next town
Where I will trade a wooden spoon
I carved myself from a branch
I found in the forest
For a doll you knitted using the wool
From your nan's old worn sweater,
I will love the doll and keep her
As my traveling companion
Until I come upon a little girl
Crying beside the road,
I will give her the doll in exchange for a smile,
A smile that takes up less room
In my shell of a home anyway.
Soon I will trade that smile for a spool of thread
To mend the hole in my pocket
The pocket in which I keep
Magic sticks and serious stones
The pocket that holds sweets

For the children who follow me,
Clambering for a story or a song.
On cold wet evenings I will climb inside my shell,
And wrap myself in memories
I will sleep the sleep of the well-content.

This is another piece from a photograph – a family of Travellers in front of their caravans. I've always been prone to "wanderlust". Let me go, just go, to places unknown.

gobnait goes galactic

A novel inspired by prompts

gobnait is abducted by her cats, who are actually aliens - Her best friend, Caireen, tags along for the fun of it. Featuring magic rocks, a doorbell, and The Listowel Races.

The border is here because printer is being obnoxious + only prints center picture

"Touch"

42

In the Forest

She sat naked on a rock dangling her swollen feet in the cool water of the lake. Her clothes were folded neatly beside her.

Waitressing was hard enough without having to wear tight skirts and high heels in order to appeal to the glitteratsy, the rich and the snobby. But the money was fair and the tips were great.

Even so, she had, not too long ago, considered going home to California to work in some lovely dingy diner where the people were down to earth and she could wear blue jeans and sneakers and just be herself.

She smiled. There was nothing that could send her back to the States now.

Here she had found a part of herself that she hadn't known existed. She laughed at the thought. How could she have known, that hidden in the Alpine wilderness above the lake-side resort she would find an intense sense of belonging.

She lifted her face to the breeze and breathed in the scent of trees and flowers and forest creatures.

Then she saw what she had been waiting for, the soft glow of the moon on the horizon. She shivered and hugged herself, rubbing her hands over the soft grey fur beginning to sprout from her arms as the moon rose full and round. Oh, it was heaven, the softness, the warmth, the feeling of power growing in her body.

She crouched on the rock, wagging her tail, and howling into the sky.

The answering howls of her pack sounded far up the mountain. Leaping through the forest she joined them, frolicking with them through the night.

It was her whole life in that single night. Tomorrow she would return to the human world, but this one night was worth everything.

She was loved. She was accepted without question. When it was time for her to leave them they bade her farewell, knowing she would return to them at the next full moon.

The prompt was "Lake Como." This is the kind of prompt I DON'T live for. Lake Como is a resort area in Italy, the kind of place I have absolutely no interest in. But I'm a good girl and I do what I'm told (occasionally) so I did a little research about the area to see what I could find out. Seems that there are (or once were) bears on one side of the lake and wolves on the other. Hmmm... It turned out to be one of my favourite stories.

From a Fighting Words Story

Love in the Time of Covid

A little old woman and a little old man
Sat dozing in their chairs one day.
Said the little old man to the little old woman
"Sure wish this pandemic would go away."

"Oh yes," said she to the little old man,
"Ah, to once again be free
To go down the town or over the hill
Or just out for a cup of tea."

They sat for a moment and thought of the times
When once they were out in the world.
Oh the fun they had as they wandered around
When he was a lad and she was a girl.

"Remember the castle," said he with a smile.
"I remember," said she with a grin.
"We never spoke of what we did there
When we couldn't find room at the inn."

"And the night in the pub in Knocknagoshel!
What a marvellous time we had.
We sang and we laughed and downed a few pints –
Got a lift home from a friendly lad.

"He drove the curves of every boreen
As fast as a fox in the hunt.
When we asked him to slow, just a wee little bit,
His laugh was more of a grunt."

"But we got home alive," said the little old man.
"We certainly did," began she,
"And now when we travel out of Listowel
In a taxi is where we'll be."

"And the day of the races in Finucane's," he began,
"Remember the man with the pipe.
He sat in the window a-tapping his foot.
He sat there the whole of the night."

"I was sure he was a leprechaun
And his pockets were full of gold.
Let's ask him you said, so that's what we did
Back then we were oh so bold."

"We approached and asked that man with the pipe
If he was a leprechaun.
From his pocket he took a little gold coin
And before our eyes he was gone.

"We heard him laugh as he faded away
And from that day to this we've been blessed
With good fortune and luck and all that is good
And all in the world that is best."

The little old man and the little old woman
Sat for a moment or two
And treasured the thoughts they had of the past,
And all that they had been through.

They dozed and they smiled at the good times they'd had
And the good times they'd have once again,
Together they dreamed of a world born anew
On the day of the pandemic's end.

This one is a little longer because we were meeting on Zoom and had fewer people, so more time. It's also a true story.

Nesting Bird

GODZILLA'S MOTHER

Old Woman in the Window

Old Woman in the Window
I see them giving me the side-eye
As they walk by my window.
I can hear them thinking,
Poor old woman,
The world has passed her by.
She has nothing more to live for
Except sit in her rickety house
And envy the young people
As they go about their lives.

Oh, if they only knew.
If they only knew that
I have lived more lives than most
Of them can even imagine.
I have climbed mountains
I have seen miracles
I have loved and been loved
And I have had friends
Who cherished my very being.

As I sit here in my window
Reflecting on my life
I pray for these young people
To grasp life with both hands
And dance boldly into the future.

This was a visual prompt. We were to find an old black and white photograph and write something about it. Since the photo I used isn't mine, I won't include it. Instead I have drawn a picture of me in the window.

52

Strolling Through the Park

Falling is one of my many talents. I don't do it particularly often, but when I do, the results are spectacular. I once fell face forward into a display of decorative rocks at a motel. Broke my glasses, scratched up my face. Just lovely. And then there was the time I tripped over the dog, hit my right eye on the door jamb and sported a colourfully decorated face for a month. But this latest one was the most interesting of all.

I was strolling through the park on a warm sunny day. Being a little old lady who has an inclination to be unsteady on her feet, I am always accompanied by Lola-Lena, also known as Little Old Lady Accessory. In other words, my trusty walker.

I was strolling along, watching the clouds, singing with birds, and not paying attention to what my feet were doing – never a good thing for a little old lady. Then I tripped on a rock.

Lola-Lena went flying ahead of me and I went crashing to the ground. My face greeting the pavement with a thud. I think I blacked out for a while.

Just so you know, although I'm really good at falling, I'm not so good at getting up. And, of course, the park was empty. Not a soul in sight.

I rolled onto the grass and was biding my time by admiring the daisies and the dandelions. I lay patiently waiting for heroes or guardian angels to rescue me.

Then I noticed that I had company.

A little brown worm was looking at me.

"Hello Worm," I said.

"Hello," said the worm. "I am not a worm."

"You look like a worm," I said.

"Looks, as you may know, can be deceiving."

"You still look like a worm," I said.

"Indeed," said the worm. "I was once only a lowly worm, like all the others, content to eat dirt and poop it out, making the world a better place for all involved. But then… but then one night I had a dream…"

"Oh, do tell," I said, as I lifted my head and rested it on my hand. "I love a good story."

"I dreamed I was a dragon, big and fierce. I grew wings and feet – I actually had feet with toes and everything! And I could fly! I could look down from the sky and see the worms crawling in the dirt, worms like I used to be."

"You still look like a worm," I said, "Perhaps, since you can speak, an overperforming worm, but a worm nonetheless."

"No," said the worm, "I am a dragon. I am only waiting for the right crusade to sprout my wings and feet – feet with toes – and perform a daring deed, perhaps rescue a damsel in distress."

My eyes lit up.

"I am," began I " currently a damsel in distress. Could you turn into a dragon and help me up?"

"You don't look like a damsel," said the worm. "You look like a little old lady."

"And you still look like a worm."

"You are being offensive," said the worm.

"You started it!" I said.

"No, you did!" retorted the worm.

"Did not."

"Did too."

"Did not."

Suddenly a pair of boots appeared before my face.

"Missus, are you OK?"

Still being in a bad mood from the current discussion with the worm I retorted, "Do I look OK?"

"Ah ya poor ol' thing, your face is all bruised. Here, let me help you up. Can you stand? Is this your walker?"

Realising I was talking to a human, I pulled myself together and let the gentleman help me up. I brushed myself off and said "Thank you so much."

He tipped his hat to me and turned to go.

Then he turned back.

"Who were you talking to down there? You were chatting away like and it sounded like you were getting all hot and bothered,"

I smiled.

"It was just a worm. A worm who thought he was a dragon."

His eyes narrowed as he looked at me. Then he smiled.

"Ah," he said. "I thought you looked familiar. You're that American storyteller, aren't you?"

"I am," said I. "I am."

As the gentleman walked away I leaned slightly closer to the ground and whispered, "Just so you know, WORM, dragons are the bad guys. They don't save people."

And I toddled down the path quickly while I still had the last word.

---

www.what3words.com is an app that has divided the entire world into 3 metre squares according to address. I used "24711 Ave 14 ½, Madera, California", one of my childhood addresses that no longer exists, and found the words outperform, dragon, worms. Supposedly, this method has greater accuracy in finding a location than postcodes or GPS. Some say not. But I don't care because I only use it for storytelling.

Ballad of the Blue-Eyed Bullfrog

Letting my pen wander wherever (I just noticed that it seems to have turned into a bird of some kind.)

Janis

It isn't fair, it just isn't fair. Mama said if I was good she'd let me go to the concert. She even let Vicki and Gracie spend the night so we could all go together. But now she says no. She said Vicki and Gracie should go without me.

She's in one of her moods. How have I not been good? This afternoon she had a migraine so I was very quiet. I polished the furniture. She's mad because I didn't vacuum. But I'm not supposed to vacuum when she has a headache.

I just can't do anything right.

Vicki and Gracie are gone. They just left.

My brother Kenny's friends picked him up and he stuck his tongue out at me as they drove away.

Kenny never does anything around the house but he gets to do whatever he wants. Mama says it's because he's 17 and I'm only 15. Also, he's a boy.

I go to my room to sulk. Daddy opens the door and peeks in. "You alright Pumpkin?"

"Yeah," I say, but I'm not.

Daddy sits down on the bed next to me.

"You really want to go, don't you."

I roll my swollen eyes at him and grunt. What a stupid question.

"Well, put your jacket on. I'll drive you."

OMG OMG OMG! I get to go to my first concert!

On the half hour drive to Fresno I keep shaking my head in disbelief.

I'm going to see Janis Joplin.

Daddy pulls up in front of the Rainbow Ballroom and I wave to Vicki and Gracie standing in line. Kenny sees my, but he ignores me. He doesn't want to be seen with his little sister.

And then I AM STANDING INSIDE!

It is everything I hoped it would be. We sit on the floor very near the front. Janis bursts onto the stage and sings 'Down on Me'. She looks into the audience and I wave at her. She gives me a crooked Janis Joplin smile.

Janis Joplin smiled at me!

I get up to dance at the back of the room. I am totally in heaven

Then I hear a commotion

"Sing 'Ball and Chain'" someone shouts from the audience.

It's my brother.

Of course it's Kenny. He never goes anywhere without causing trouble. "Sing 'Ball and Chain'", he shouts again. He begins to chant: "Ball and Chain, Ball and Chain, Ball and Chain!"

Janis scowls at him. I can see her hackles rise as she throws the microphone down and steps towards the edge of the stage.

OMG! Was I going to get to see Janis Joplin beat up my brother? Oh YES! Please, please, please let it happen.

No such luck. The bass player puLLs Janis back. The audience applauds. I stick my tongue out at Kenny as security escorts him out the door.

I continue dancing.

It is the most wonderful night.

Janus is the two-faced god of beginnings. This story fits because Janis Joplin was my very first concert. That's my story and I'm stickin' to it.

Another Running Dream

Teacher Cranky Woman

Teacher Godfrey is REALLY grumpy today. She's being snappy with everyone, even Teacher Karen. She just passed by the table where I am playing quietly and snapped at me.

"Robbie, I gave the 5 minute warning 10 minutes ago. Put that puzzle away ... NOW."

I looked up at her and frowned. "Teacher Godfrey, I think I have a new name for you."

She scowled at me.

"Yeah, what's that?"

"I think from now on I'm gonna have to call you Teacher Cranky Woman."

She stopped.

She raised an eyebrow.

As she squinted at me the corners of her lips began to curl upwards and her eyes began to twinkle.

Then she laughed out loud.

"I deserved that Robbie."

She turned to the rest of the class and announced, "OK guys, it's story time."

Then she turned back to me and said, "But you still have to put the puzzle away – move it!"

The prompt was "another speaker's voice".

Bianca and the Bubbles

Everything I learned about science I learned in preschool. It wasn't until I began my 25 year career as a preschool teacher that I learned how much fun science could be.

Children want to KNOW things and it was my job to help them find answers.

Bubbles! A subject near and dear to the hearts of almost every child I've ever known. And many adults, too

A four year old once asked me why she couldn't make bubbles with just plain water. I said, "of course you can. ALL you have to do is mix water with air." I took her to the sink, and filled it with water. I turned the tap on high and lo and behold, there were bubbles, tiny little bubbles

"But I can't blow those in the air."

"To make a round bubble that floats in the air," I told her, "you have to mix the water with soap."

"But how does soap and water make bubbles."

"Well, you use the little wand and you blow into the soapy water and the air gets caught inside the soap and that makes a bubble. It's like when you wash dishes and you turn the water on and the falling water pushes air into the dish soap and it makes bubbles."

"How does it make a bubble?"

"It has something to do with molecules."

"What's a molecule?"

"Well, it's, ah, it's one of the little things that make up everything. Different kinds of molecules make up different things."

"I thought atoms make up everything."

(Smart kid.)

"Well molecules are made up of atoms. Atoms are smaller."

"What do they look like?"

"Um, they're too small to see."

"Then how do we know they're there?"

"Scientists find them. They use really powerful microscopes."

"I have a microscope but I don't see atoms, or even molecules. I only see parts of worms."

"The ones that scientists use are way more powerful than yours."

"I want one of those."

"They cost a lot of money. Maybe you can get one when you grow up and become a scientist."

"Yeah, I wanna be a scientist when I grow up. Or a jellyfish. They're pretty."

Bianca ran off to play.

I loved being a preschool teacher!

The prompt was "soap and water".

66

The Robin

It was lying on the grass, not moving. The little girl squatted down next to it to get a good look. It was so pretty, the tiny red feathers on the breast, the white on its belly, and the grey-brown feathers on the back and tail.

She reached down and lightly poked it.

It moved.

"You're still alive," said the little girl, smiling, and she picked it up, gently curling her fingers around its still warm body. The robin shuddered, opened its eyes, and for a brief moment they looked at each other. Then the little robin gave a deep sigh, closed its eyes, and died.

The little girl sat down on the rustling leaves and cuddled the robin to her breast.

As she did so, there was a wisp of a breeze that rustled its feathers. As she looked down at it lying in her hand she thought she saw its spirit rise from its body and disperse, like dandelion fluff, in the air. The spirit was gone but she still held the body in her hands.

She picked up a stick to dig a hole. She didn't like the thought of the poor little thing lying in the freezing dirt, so she looked around. There were dry leaves. There were sticks. She could weave a little basket with sticks and grass, but that would take time. She looked up and could see her friends playing in the distance.

She put her hand in her pocket and pulled out a rock, a marble, an éclair and a dinosaur. But in her other pocket was the handkerchief given to her by her nana. It was soft, white linen, with a sunflower embroidered in one corner. She sighed. She would like to keep it, but knew Nana would approve of giving it to the robin.

She wrapped the robin in the handkerchief and lowered it gently into the hole, covering it with earth and leaves.

Standing and wiping her hands on her jacket, she said, "Bye-bye little birdie," paused for a moment and ran off to play.

The prompt was "white linen". Linen is a symbol of purity and was also used as a burial cloth.

Sitting on a wall watching

nothing happen.

70

The True Story of Rumpelstilskin

The little man sat in the corner behind the pile of straw and thought, There she sits, poor child, weeping so prettily. Shall I help? She did after all get herself into this mess, telling her father to tell the king that she could spin straw into gold. Look at those soft hands – she's never spun anything into anything in her life. He chuckled softly.

"Who's there?"

He crept out of his corner and bowed. "Hello dearie. Why are you weeping so?

"Who are you?"

"A friend my pet, a friend, here to assist you if you have need. How may I serve you?" He bowed but she drew away in disgust at his misshapen countenance.

She bit her lip as she replied, "I am to spin this straw into gold. I don't know how to spin anything. My father, the miller, has prepared me for a royal marriage, not a life of drudgery."

"Oh that's no bother my pretty. And if I do this for you perhaps you will give me some small token in appreciation?"

The young woman snatched the pendant from her neck and threw it at his feet, thinking, There will be more jewels when I marry the king.

She dried her tears, sat up as straight as she could on the little stool and said in a regal manner, "You may begin."

He picked up the bauble, placed it in his satchel and began to spin.

By morning the room was full of gold, but the king was not satisfied and demanded that another room of straw be spun into gold again – and yet again on the next day.

The third time the little man asked for payment, the young woman protested. "I have nothing more to give you. When I am queen I will have more jewels. You will have to wait."

"And wait I will, but I have no need of more jewels," said he, and he thought, Let us see how strong is her determination to be queen.

"Perhaps you will bequeath to me your firstborn child when you are married to the king?"

He could see the wheels of her mind turning. Perhaps there would be no child, or maybe the child would be born dead, as so many were in these days. She would take the chance. After all, she wouldn't be queen at all if she didn't produce another room of gold.

So the little man spun and spun the night long and in the morning the king was at last satisfied.

The king and the miller's daughter were married and soon thereafter, a child was born. The king, however, was not pleased. A son and heir was needed, not this girl-child.

72

The queen stamped her foot and sulked in her royal chambers as the babe wailed in the cradle beside her. Why could the screaming brat not be a boy?

How could she be rid of it?

"Wait! That ugly little man. I must keep my royal promise! If he wants this, this, thing, then he shall have her."

She called her servants and bid them search in the hills and forests far and wide for the grotesque little dwarf.

They found him deep in the woods, sitting peacefully beside the fire in front of his small cottage.

"The queen has summoned you," they announced as they seized him and hauled him to the palace.

He was taken to the nursery where he found the queen roughly jostling the crying baby in her arms.

"Ah yes," he said as he bowed. "We had a bargain, did we not? Are you prepared to give me the babe?

" Yes," she said, "you wanted my firstborn, here it is. Take it away."

The little man paused. "You will really give me this child?"

"Yes. Take it." She pushed the baby into his arms, turned, and strode out of the room.

As soon as the child was placed in his arms she stopped crying as she had cried nonstop since the day she was born. She began to gurgle and coo as she reached up to touch the face above her.

The ugly little man looked at the child lovingly and said, "My name is Rumpelstiltskin. When you are old enough you will tell me the name by which you would like to be called. Until then I will simply call you Love."

Tenderly cradling the child, he disappeared into the forest.

Life went on in the palace, but, sadly, the king and queen were not blessed with another child, and when they died, leaving no heir, the kingdom fell to ruin.

But high atop a wooded mountain, a young girl blossomed in the beauty of goodness and kindness, carefully and lovingly tended by her father, whom she loved dearly, and thought the most handsome creature in the forest.

The assignment was to write a fairy-tale from the villain's point of view. But was Rumpelstiltskin really a villain? I say not. He was odd-looking and therefore suspect. I've always had an affinity for those who don't fit into society and Rumpelstiltskin has always been one of my favourites. Also, he has the coolest name.

Walk a Mile

I once was young and now I'm not.
If you were to try to walk
A mile in my shoes these days
You wouldn't get far
Unless...
Unless you were to step
Into my past.
Oh, and then the places you'd go,
The things you'd see
And good lord
The things you'd do.
It would make you wonder
How I'm still in the land of the living.
Yes, I'm too old and rumpty
To wander far these days.
But I wandered when I could
And I took my chances
And I had my fun.
I regret nothing.
Now I sit in a comfy chair

With two dogs on my lap
To keep me warm
And Himself across the room
To make me laugh
And roses in the garden
And apple trees outside the door.
However, my friends,
I'm not done yet
My shoes won't take me
Far these days
But my mind is
Away with the fairies
And we are having a blast.

The prompt was "walk a mile in my shoes," but, truth be told, I don't even like to wear shoes. I'm just another old hippie.

Mama Bear's porridge
was Just Right.
6 January 2025

Monkey crashes the car

A Step too Far

There is no door, there is no gate.
Nothing to separate this world
from that world,
except a circular mound of earth.
There is a quiet within,
a quiet loud enough
to be heard from where I stand
on the outside of
the woodland temple.
I hesitate, but only briefly,
as I step across the threshold
into the world of the Fey.

Be careful, I have been told.
They are mischievous.
They are tricky.
You may never return.
Ah, but I am well-acquainted
With tricksters, although I am
from a land far away.

79

I am of the land
of Coyote and Raven.
I have stood before
Coyote on the mountain
as Raven circled above us.
"If Coyote looks at you,"
I was told,
"Don't look back."

So what did I do?
I looked straight
into the eyes of the trickster
and she looked into mine,
nodding in recognition.

Is it bravery or hubris
to think I am one of them
and will be accepted
as such?

There may be danger
within the Fairy Circle
but I will step lightly
into the rath
with a smile on my lips.

If I never return
you will know
I have taken
a step too far.

"A step too far" was the prompt (I think).

80

My Lips Are Sealed

So quiet. So, so quiet. I hadn't heard this much silence since – well, since this time last year.

During the day the campground had been alive with the sound of hammering and sawing and raking, with the occasional sound of a chainsaw as a damaged tree was cut down. The cabins were nearly ready for the influx of campers during the Memorial Day Weekend.

But now that the crew had all gone home there was just me. Just me and the silence, the silence and I. Silence.

It was amazing and wonderful that they allowed me to rent a cabin here before the campground was open. For a week I could escape the job and the city. It was heaven.

My campfire was blazing in the fire pit. I was very proud of my fire. Pretty damned good for a city girl.

I read until the dark settled in. Then I simply sat, enjoying the silence and the darkness. Lovely peaceful darkness.

Little night creatures began to stir in the forest around me. People at work often asked me, "Aren't you afraid out there at night in the mountains all by yourself?"

As far as I was concerned, there was nothing to be afraid of. No bears had been seen near the camp in almost ten years.

Mountain lions probably wouldn't come near the fire. The only creatures who would cause me concern were humans wandering around in the night, but I honestly didn't even give that much thought, not way out there on the mountain.

No, I am quite comfortable in the mountains, in the dark, surrounded by the silence of the forest.

I sipped my beer as my eyes slowly closed and I fell asleep, mesmerized by the flames.

Then I dreamed.

I dreamed that the silence was broken by the sound of something creeping by on the crackling twigs and leaves.

I dreamed that a shadow passed between me and the fire.

I dreamed I heard the "psst" of a tab being pulled from a beer can.

I opened my eyes.

The creature smiled at me.

It lifted the beer can in salute, and said, "I hope you don't mind. I got thirsty."

The creature was huge, as tall as the cabin, with shaggy greenish-brown hair, the color of the forest.

It sat down cross-legged on the other side of the fire pit and sipped its beer.

It smiled and cocked one eye at me. "You haven't screamed yet."

"Um, well, nobody is close enough to hear me scream," I said, "so what would be the point?"

It threw its head back and laughed.

"Good point, but most people are so shocked to see me they don't think of that." It paused. "I was going to say 'women,' but, truth be told, the men scream just as loud."

"Are you what I think you are?"

"First of all, I'm a 'who', not a 'what,' and before you ask, I'm a 'she' not a 'he'. So, who do you think I am?"

"Bigfoot."

She grimaced. "We prefer to be called Sasquatch. Bigfoot is considered rather rude and a bit disrespectful."

"Sorry."

She took another swig of her beer.

"Would you like another one?" I asked.

She grinned. "Thought you'd never ask."

I pulled out another couple of beers and handed her one.

She took a sip and said, "Y'know, you can't tell anyone about this. We don't want a bunch of crypto zoologists and sightseers invading our space."

"My lips are sealed. No one would believe me anyway."

"Probably not. But most people try."

"I'm a storyteller and nobody believes most of what I tell them anyway," I laughed.

She sat up straight, eyes wide. "A storyteller you say? I have often sat hidden in the trees during human summer camps, listening to the stories they tell around the fire. Could you tell me a story? Do you know the story of Wiley and the Hairy Man. That's always been one of my favorites."

She leaned forward and gazed at me over the fire as I began:

"Wiley lived down along the banks of the Tom Bigbee River, with his Mama, who warned him 'NEVER go out into the swamps all by yourself 'cause the Hairy Man lives out there and the Hairy Man'll get you if you don't watch out.'"

She closed her eyes and smiled in contentment.

The prompt was "my lips are sealed".

Monday 3 February 2025
I dreamed I was making a quilt from my old dresses.

85

Conversations With God

"I'd rather be a swallow than a snail," I told God.

She said "I've already chosen your next form."

"Don't I have anything to say about it?"

"Last time I let you choose for yourself you chose cockroach. That didn't go too well."

"Yeah, well I thought cockroaches were pretty indestructible – they say they can survive a nuclear war."

"They do fine as long as they don't get stepped on." She paused. "So," she continued, "what did you learn from your experience as a cockroach?"

"I learned it's safer to stay under the woodwork and not go running around in the open."

God laughed and shook her head. "Nope. That wasn't it."

"Then what was I supposed to learn?"

"You know I can't tell you that. You have to learn it on your own." She paused. "Have you ever considered going back as a human?"

"What? No, no, no! I'm certainly not ready for that. Humans are scary. They're evil. They're stupid."

Mami Wata floated into the room, leaving a trail of water droplets behind her. She went to God's computer in the corner and began tapping keys, soaking the keyboard.

God asked, "What are you looking for?"

"Don't you have the files on Manimekhala?"

"I sent them over to you last night. Please," said God, taking the keyboard out of Mami's hands. "Please leave my computers alone."

Mami Wata said "Humph." Then noticed me sitting on the footstool.

"Oh, are you ready for your next life already? I thought you just went back."

"I did, but I didn't last very long. I got squished right away."

She laughed. "Maybe you should go back as a mermaid. We know how to have fun." She grinned. "And we never get squished."

"Maybe not, but I have a friend who went as a mermaid and she got eaten by a shark."

"Well, I warned her that they don't like it when you pull their tail fins." Mami Wata turned and drizzled out of the room.

Olowlowishkya stuck his head in the door. "You almost done in here? Odin is calling an emergency meeting over in Valhalla. Don't know what it's about. He said he needs you to be there."

God sighed and stood up. "Shiva must be on the rampage again." She walked to the door. "Oh, I almost forgot," She waved her hand towards me. "Have fun."

In an instant I transformed.

"Oh shit," I muttered from inside the egg. "Not a hagfish again!"

Mami Wata (Mother Water) encompasses worship of a group of water spirits in South East Nigeria. Manimekhala is goddess of lightning and the seas in many countries of South East Asia. Olowlowishkya is another name for Kokopeli, the Hopi trickster god who teaches us how NOT to behave.

About the Author

Godfrey Coppinger was born a very long time ago in the far away land of California, a place she didn't particularly want to be.

So, when she got old enough to leave home, she did. Her destination was the wilds of Wyoming where she wandered the mountains between Cheyenne and Laramie. She spent two winters there, trying not to break the frozen sheets when she took them off the line.

She soon got fed up with that and travelled to Oregon on a whim. She often did things on a whim.

Oregon was it. Oregon was home, the place she had always wanted to be, even though she didn't know it. In that wonderful land she made art, wrote words, made music and told stories.

Storytelling was the making of her. She was accepted into the Eastern Oregon Artists in the Schools Program. She taught storytelling in eight schools, two weeks at a time.

During the first month she made half her yearly income! (Artists, buskers, and storytellers aren't known for being wealthy.) She considered the possibilities. She could live comfortably for a while, or she could have an adventure.

She chose adventure.

She arrived in Ireland on May, 19, 1984, her 33rd birthday. She stayed at a lovely B&B in Dungarvan. On the telly she saw Gay Byrne talking to John B. Keane about Writers' Week.

Three days later she sat on a stool in John B. Keane's pub. Mary Keane was behind the bar. The television was on: *Knight Rider*.

"What percentage of programs on Irish TV are American?" She asked.

"I'm not sure," replied Mary. "I don't watch it, myself. Perhaps the gentleman sitting next to you might know."

She turned and looked at the curly headed young man on the stool next to her.

It was no gentleman! It was Himself, the one who does not wish to be named. As it turned out, that 'gentleman' ruined her whole vacation – so she had to marry him and ruin the rest of his life to get even.

He tells her she's doing an excellent job.

The lived together on O'Connell's Avenue then returned to California in 1990. There Himself found the perfect job working for an ice company. They gave him a truck to drive and he wandered the San Joaquin Valley fixing ice boxes and conversing with the locals.

As for Godfrey, she discovered the joy of teaching preschool, a job in which she sang songs, told stories, wrote words, played with children and had a wonderful time. And every two weeks they gave her money that she didn't even have to ask for! Life could not have been better.

But it did get better. Upon retirement Godfrey and Himself returned to Ireland and are happily ensconced in a tiny home with two dogs at the edge of Listowel.

She now spends her days writing more words and drawing lots of silly pictures.

Godfrey is determined to NEVER MOVE AGAIN!

Listowel is, like it or not, stuck with her.

In memoriam, Geraldine Serpa Chapman